To George Pack with love from
Ian

To Luther, Jack and Daisy, Kiki, Za-Za, Percy and Peter
Jude

First published in 2002 in Great Britain by Gullane Children's Books
This paperback edition published in 2002 by

Winchester House, 259-269 Old Marylebone Road,
London NW1 5XJ

1 3 5 7 9 10 8 6 4 2

A CIP record for this title is available from the British Library.

ISBN 1-86233-378-5 hb
ISBN 1-86233-470-6 pb

Printed and bound in China

Go To Bed, Doodlehead!

Ian Whybrow • Jude Wisdom

There once was a cat
With a face like that –
Everyone called him
grumpy cat . . .

And I will tell you why.

He did a lot of

bouncing

and ***racing***

and **pouncing**

and ***chasing***

and he **never**
went to bed at
Proper Bed Time.

So every morning,
he woke up tired.
He washed, he dressed
and he put on his
grrrrumpy face.

Grumpy
SAD
Happy

Dog came to visit.
He brought Cat
some breakfast.

"Oh, foo! Fish flakes **again!**" grumbled Cat.
He ate two spoonfuls and snapped,

"No More Now!"

"Will you have
one more little
spoonful,
just for me?"
asked Dog.

"No!
Go away,
Poodlehead!"
yowled Cat.

"Oh wuff! What a **Sour Puss!**"

said Dog. "I'll go and tell Chicken.
Maybe she can cheer Cat up."

Chicken came round to play.
"Hello Cat," she said. "Let's play Henhouse."
"No! Push off, Peckyface!" spat Cat.

"Oh cluck! What a **Moody Mog**!"
said Chicken. "I'll go and tell Giraffe.
Maybe he can cheer Cat up."

Giraffe
came round
to tell Cat one
of his jokes.
*"What do
ghosties eat?"*

"**Buzz
off,**
Big Spots!"
hissed Cat.

"Oh gosh! What a Grumpy Cat!"

said Giraffe. "I think I'll have a good talk to the others about this."

Giraffe and Chicken and Dog got together.
They had a **Hum** and they had a **Ha**,
and then they had an idea.

That evening,
they all
dropped in for a
Sleepover Party.

They had pizza
with Special
Sardine Topping.

They had **bouncing** and *racing*

and **pouncing** and ***chasing***

and **then . . .**

They played
Go To Bed, Doodlehead!
Giraffe read them a nice tall story, then they turned off the light . . .

. . . and went to sleep at Proper Bed Time!

Next morning, Cat got up not feeling tired at all. Instead of putting on his **grumpy** face . . .

. . . he put on his **happy** face!

At breakfast, Cat smiled at Dog and said,
"Oh, Fish flakes! **Myum myum!**"
And he ate them **all** up.

When Chicken wanted to play,
he smiled and he purred,
"Yes, let's play Henhouse! Hooray!"
And he played nicely till noon.

When Giraffe told him a joke, he laughed and laughed and told him a joke back.

"Why are Smiley Cats the best? Because they are ***purrrrfect!***"

Joke
Book

And do you know what, every evening after that, Cat played

Go To Bed, Doodlehead!

He read a story,
turned off the light
and went to sleep at
Proper Bed Time.

So what did everybody
call him now?
Did they call him
Grumpy Cat?
No.

They called him . . . **Smiley Cat!**

The cat who loved to play *Go To Bed, Doodlehead!*